THE RAID

Rachel McLean writes thrillers that make your pulse race and your brain tick. Originally a self-publishing sensation, she has sold millions of copies digitally, with massive success in the UK, and a growing reach internationally. She is the author of the Dorset Crime novels and the spin-off McBride & Tanner series and Cumbria Crime series. In 2021, she won the Kindle Storyteller Award with *The Corfe Castle Murders* and her books regularly hit No 1 in the Bookstat ebook chart on launch.

Joel Hames is a Lancashire-based writer of crime fiction, and the editor of million-selling books across multiple genres. Joel's own works include the Dead North series featuring lawyer Sam Williams, and the psychological thriller *The Lies I Tell*. Most recently, he has been working with titan of crime fiction Rachel McLean on the hugely successful Cumbria Crime series.

ALSO BY RACHEL MCLEAN AND JOEL HAMES

Cumbria Crime series

The Harbour
The Mine
The Cairn
The Barn
The Lake
The Wood
...and more to come

RACHEL McLEAN & JOEL HAMES

CUMBRIA CRIME NOVELLA

THE RAID

Copyright © 2024 by Rachel McLean and Joel Hames

All rights reserved.

No part of this book may be reproduced in any form or by any electronic or mechanical means, including information storage and retrieval systems, without written permission from the author, except for the use of brief quotations in a book review.

This is a work of fiction. Names, characters, businesses, places, events and incidents are either the products of the author's imagination or used in a fictitious manner. Any resemblance to actual persons, living or dead, or actual events is purely coincidental.

Ackroyd Publishing

ackroydpublishing.com

Printed and bound in the UK by CPI Group (Uk) Ltd, Croydon CR0 4YY

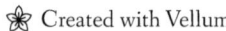 Created with Vellum

AUTHOR'S NOTE

The Raid is set before the fourth book in the Cumbria Crime series.
Happy reading!
Rachel McLean

CHAPTER ONE

"What's your name?" asked the man opposite Sue.

It was dark in here, on the first floor, and although they weren't wearing masks, Sue couldn't see his face clearly under his pointy hat. He'd already been there when she'd arrived, so she hadn't been able to get a decent look at him walking in, either.

Her own age, she guessed. Maybe a little younger.

"My real name?"

"No, no, I mean – I mean your name for this."

"Marston," she said. Outside, there was something that might have been an angry roar, followed by the sound of people cheering.

"Marston," he repeated. "They didn't give you a first name, then?"

"They didn't think a man's name would be appropriate, and they didn't think a woman's name would be historically accurate."

"So it's just Marston, then. I'm Alexander Milton."

He stood, walked across, and offered his hand. She shook it.

"Shall we make up a name for you? It feels weird, calling you Marston."

"Well, I don't mind telling you my real name. It's not as if we're spies or anything."

'Alexander Milton' swivelled his head from side to side dramatically. "No, I suppose we're not. The only traitor, if the history books are telling the truth, is on the other side."

"David Freeman," she said.

"You know your history, Marston."

"Sue," she corrected. "And no, but I make it a point to read up on these activities."

"I don't think I've seen you at one of these before."

The same story. The same explanation. It became boring after a while.

"I've only recently moved to Whitehaven. I've done a lot of live-action roleplay back in Liverpool, but this is my first one here."

"You're from Liverpool?" he asked, with what sounded like surprise. She was used to that, too.

"Wirral. And no, I don't have much of an accent. What's that?"

The noises outside had grown closer, and now they could hear it clearly, just below them. She checked her watch. Nine thirty-three.

Just a few minutes late, then.

She waited, and then the voices moved away. Someone shouted. Someone sang. Someone, she thought, was vomiting, but that might have been her imagination.

A lot of people seemed to be using the re-enactment of John Paul Jones's raid on Whitehaven as an excuse to get

CHAPTER ONE

drunk. And given what had actually happened first time around, that wasn't entirely unreasonable.

From further away came more shouts. Someone screaming, possibly. Were they getting carried away? Hopefully, they wouldn't forget the whole point of the evening.

More voices, closer now. Stopping under the window again.

"Be careful when you're in there," said a voice on the edge of hearing.

"We know what we're doing, Captain Jones," said another, much louder.

"I'm quite sure you do," agreed the first man, 'Captain Jones'. "But please bear in mind that this is an office. A workplace. I don't want anything damaged or lost." There was a certain pompousness to his voice that set Sue's teeth on edge. She didn't like any of them.

"This is the wrong sort of gun," said a woman.

"No, it's not," replied another man. "If you've done your reading, you'll know that these are decent reproductions of the weapons carried by Jones's men."

"If you've done your reading," mimicked the woman. "I've done plenty of reading. As you know."

There was a clattering noise. The ladders being positioned. Sue glanced at the window, which was closed but not locked.

The first man spoke again. "Ladies and gentlemen, if we're to preserve any sense of accuracy, I should be grateful if you'd keep your voices down."

There was a general grumbling, and he went on.

"It's bad enough that we're having to use my office because the original fort isn't here. And it's bad enough that we're having to use ladders. But at the very least, let's not try to alert the guards upstairs."

Sue stifled a laugh. Her companion, 'Alexander Milton', chortled out loud for a second before he managed to silence himself.

She'd been aware this was an office, although the room they were in, on the first floor, was dusty and bore few signs of recent use. She'd been shown in downstairs and ushered up, hastily, then left to her own devices. Which was fair enough. As one of the guards who were to be surprised and captured by Jones and his men climbing through the window, she didn't have much of a role in the event.

But that didn't mean she couldn't enjoy it.

More shouts from outside, further away. Back in the eighteenth century, half of Jones's men had gone to the pub instead of advancing the cause of American independence by burning the harbour. It sounded like their modern-day equivalents were following their example. And the man playing Jones might complain about using a ladder, but the American sailors had probably been less stout than their re-enactors. Climbing up on each other's shoulders would have been a recipe for disaster.

"Carefully now," she heard. 'Captain Jones' again. Then more clattering, more muttered arguments, and a scraping noise. A minute later, the window was open, and they were in.

There were five of them. It was dark anyway, but the raiders were wearing a variety of masks that might have been bought for a Hallowe'en party, for all the resemblance they bore to the disguises Jones's men would have worn.

Would Jones's men have bothered with disguises? She didn't think so. But it was all fun.

"We surrender," said her colleague. Someone approached her, a slight figure. She made to stand, but the person in front of her waved her back down, and, moving with surprising dexterity, tied her to the chair.

"Is that really necessary?" she asked.

"Sorry," said 'Captain Jones', whose office they were apparently using.

"Hang on," said her companion, 'Alexander Milton'. "Not me. I've got to head off in a minute."

"Fair enough," said someone, and Sue found herself wishing she'd thought of that. She feared she had a long and boring evening ahead of her.

"Can you just loosen these?" she asked, but no one seemed to hear her.

And suddenly, she was alone.

She listened as the footsteps receded. Would anyone remember she'd been left here?

She pulled experimentally against the ropes, but they were too tight. She couldn't even reach her phone.

The whole thing had been over in less than five minutes, and it had been dark and confusing. A blur. This wasn't as much fun as she'd hoped.

There was a thud from outside.

From outside the room. Inside the building. What was that?

She listened. Footsteps. Above her. She closed her eyes and tried to remember the building from the outside. Light blue paintwork, the shade they went in for around here. Several floors.

There was someone on the second floor. But all the raiders should have left by now.

She tried to still her breathing and listened carefully. Definitely footsteps. And... was that more than one set?

Yes. Because now she could hear, indistinctly, the murmur of voices.

Then another thud. A series of thuds. On the floor above her, or the walls...

Then a voice, a shout.

There was a moment's silence, followed by the crunch of something falling in the street outside. Sue shuddered.

It was followed almost immediately by more noises from upstairs. Shuffling. Then more footsteps.

Then silence. Shouts and screams in the distance. But closer to hand, nothing.

Sue pulled against the ropes again. Still too tight.

But the chair was just a thin wooden thing.

She pressed her feet against the ground and tried to stand. The chair came up with her, but it worked.

Her feet were still tied together. It took nearly a minute, but eventually, she reached the window.

The raiders had left it open, and a cool breeze filled the room. Sue leaned forward, aware that the chair would prevent her from overbalancing and falling out of the window.

Were those more sounds, above her? She turned her head to look up, but there was nothing there. It was too dark, anyway. And she knew she was only delaying the moment she had to look down.

She looked down.

She'd known what she was about to see. Ever since she'd heard that crunch.

But knowing what she was about to see, and seeing it...

She opened her mouth and screamed.

CHAPTER ONE

There was the sound of footsteps outside. Running. Several sets. And there he was, approaching from the marina end of the street. Her fellow guard. Alexander Milton. She'd been right. He was about her age. He frowned as he ran, looking up at her, then back down at the thing he was running towards.

He'd heard her scream. Thank God.

There was another man, not far behind him. 'Captain Jones' himself.

The two of them slowed, then stopped, directly below her.

Directly over the body.

She couldn't see much of the figure lying on the ground. Just the mask. One of the raiders, then.

The man she knew as Alexander Milton pulled a phone out of his pocket and dialled a number.

"Boss," she heard. "It's Tom. I'm sorry to bother you at home, but I'm in Lowther Street. And there's a dead body here."

CHAPTER TWO

DI Zoe Finch parked further along Lowther Street. Tom had given her directions, but she knew where she was going. She'd been here before.

But everything seemed different.

There were more people on the streets than she'd ever seen here. Most of them drunk, half of them wearing costumes that she'd have been hard-pressed to identify if she hadn't known that they were re-enacting John Paul Jones's raid on Whitehaven during the American War of Independence.

From the state of them, most of the revellers probably weren't sure what they were supposed to be re-enacting anyway.

She found Tom in the road outside the office. He'd dragged a chair out of the building and shoved it in the middle of the road, to stop the traffic.

"Uniform'll be along in a minute," he told her.

"Who's the dead man?" she asked, pointing at the body on the ground. Whoever he was, he was looking up at the sky, or would have been if he hadn't been dead. Blood seeped from the back of his head. Zoe glanced up at the building. Windows were open on the first and second floors. *The second*, she imagined. *That would have been enough to kill him.*

"He's one of the raiders," Tom explained.

Raiders?

She turned to look at Tom. She wasn't going to ask him what he was wearing. She wasn't going to ask him about his pointy hat and his knee-length shirt. She wasn't going to ask him about that weird piece of cloth around his neck. Most of all, she wasn't going to ask him about...

No. They couldn't be stockings. They weren't stockings. Were they?

"What do you mean?"

Behind her, a man cleared his throat, and a familiar voice announced, "He was one of my party, DI Finch. One of John Paul Jones's plucky raiders."

She turned. She'd known she was likely to see Alistair Freeburn here. She just hadn't expected to see him wearing an ornate buttoned coat, navy blue, with a scarlet front, and gold epaulettes on the shoulders.

"We entered through the windows, as Jones's original party did, surprising the guards in the guardhouse. The original fort is no more, alas, so I've offered the use of my office, which isn't far from where the fort would have been. From here, Jones headed north—"

"With respect, Mr Freeburn, I'm not enormously interested in the details of the raid. I want to know who this man is. In real life."

"Ah."

Alistair Freeburn looked down at the dead man and

shook his head. Freeburn was an odd man in many ways, and he'd made Zoe's life difficult when she'd first run across him, but since then, and in spite of an obsession with honour and tradition that she found both tiresome and occasionally offensive, he'd been more than helpful.

And Zoe wasn't going to comment on his clothes. Or laugh at them.

There were shouts, from the marina area. More shouts from behind. Zoe turned, instinctively, and then turned back to Freeburn.

It would only be more drunk people.

"I'm sorry," Freeburn said. "I wish I knew. But although I am the co-chairman of this group, I tend to leave most of the admin to William. I didn't even know your young colleague would be joining us tonight."

Zoe turned to Tom, no more interested in the management of Alistair Freeburn's live-action roleplay group than she was in John Paul bloody Jones.

The sound of an ambulance drew near, then stopped, somewhere close by. She could see the blue lights in the sky, somewhere to the west.

"Do you know him?"

Tom shook his head.

"Sorry, boss. I've only been to a few of these things. And there are so many people here tonight."

He shrugged apologetically, and Zoe reminded herself not to mention the stockings.

"Bloody hell, look at the state of you," said a voice. "Those aren't stockings, are they?"

Zoe bit back a smile and turned to Nina.

"Good. You're here."

"I was waiting for this one in the Anchor Vaults. I— Oh."

CHAPTER TWO

She'd turned from Tom, past the dead man, to Alistair Freeburn.

"Mr Freeburn," she said. "Or do I call you Lord Admiral?"

Freeburn gave a condescending smile. "We of the free United States Navy don't hold with such things as lords, DC Kapoor," he said.

Behind them, Zoe thought she heard someone being sick.

There was too much going on. A bad night for someone to die. And a bad night for her to be one team member down. Aaron had picked an inconvenient time to be off sick.

Zoe heard footsteps, running, and turned to see a PC approaching. He stopped in front of her.

"Ma'am," he said, panting. She didn't recognise him, but there were plenty of uniformed officers she still didn't know.

At least the cavalry were here.

"Good," she said. "Tom, can you take charge of the scene? I need—"

"I'm sorry, Ma'am," said the uniform, still panting. "There's been a mugging. Just up there. Violent one. Victim's still unconscious."

He pointed towards the seafront. So that was where the ambulance had been heading.

"With respect, PC—"

"PC Harper, Ma'am."

"One crime at a time, PC Harper. We've got a dead body here. I don't think your mugging's going to trump that."

CHAPTER THREE

The whole system was creaky tonight.

At least the boss had come quickly when Tom had called. And Nina hadn't been far behind. But the pathologist, Dr Robertson, was on his way back from Manchester Airport and wouldn't be with them for a while. And when Stella Berry, the crime scene manager, had finally deigned to return Tom's call, she'd told him she'd send Huz.

Huz was good. Tom liked Huz. He was perfectly comfortable working with Huz, more comfortable than he'd have been working with Stella, in any event.

But Huz still wasn't here.

Meanwhile, Uniform were all over town, dealing with drunks and minor incidents, when Tom wanted them here, keeping the public away, helping him preserve a crime scene.

If it was a crime scene. He glanced upstairs at the open windows. It might be a crime. It might be an accident.

It was probably suicide, wasn't it?

The open window. The woman, shouting.

"There might be a witness, boss," he said, and pointed up to the first floor. "The woman I was up there with. She must have seen something."

"Why do you say that?"

"It was her screaming that made me turn back."

Leaving Nina with the body and a newly arrived PC, a lean woman with short, dark hair and a slender face, Tom led the boss upstairs. Glancing behind him, he was surprised to see Alistair Freeburn trailing up after them.

But why should he be surprised? This was Freeburn's office, after all.

Upstairs, the woman who'd referred to herself as 'Marston', and then admitted she was actually called Sue, was still sitting in the same chair. Someone, possibly Freeburn, possibly one of the Uniforms, had untied her, at least, and given her a drink. A whisky, Tom noted enviously.

"This is Alexis's office," Freeburn announced once they were all in the room. Now the lights were on you could tell it was just a normal office at a normal law firm. In the dark, waiting for people to turn up and climb in through the window, it had seemed somehow sinister.

"How is Alexis?" asked the boss, and Freeburn shook his head.

"It's not going well," he replied. "We have some hope, but one must be realistic."

Alexis? Of course. Alexis Todd. One of the other partners. The one who'd been pleasant, in contrast to Alistair Freeburn. The one who was suffering from what sounded like terminal cancer.

"Back again, Alexander Milton?"

He turned to see Sue smiling up at him. He approached,

shook her hand, and introduced her to the boss. And then, because he was still hovering, apparently unwilling to be dismissed, to Alistair Freeburn.

"We've met," Sue said, pointing to her whisky. "And it's Sue Bracewell. Not Marston."

The boss was frowning in confusion. He'd explain later.

"Can you tell me what happened?" he asked.

"It's only what I heard," Sue told him. "I didn't see anything until I looked out of the window and saw... well, saw him."

She took a sip from her glass, swallowed, and shut her eyes. Tom could almost feel the liquid sliding down her throat, the comforting heat.

Maybe he could ask Freeburn for a whisky?

"I heard these noises beforehand," Sue continued. She pointed out, towards the landing. "I heard voices. Footsteps. More than one set. And then, after the fall, more noises." She pointed up at the ceiling, and Tom heard Freeburn gasp behind him.

"That," the lawyer said, "is our library."

Before any of them had a chance to respond, Freeburn was out of the door and heading towards the staircase. Tom looked at the boss.

He was closer.

He ran after Freeburn, shouting as he went.

"Stop, Mr Freeburn. You can't go up there."

Halfway up the stairs already, Freeburn stopped and turned to him.

"Why, precisely, am I not permitted to enter my own library?"

"All of that area." Tom pointed up the stairs. "It needs to be sealed off. We need to wait for CSI to show up."

CHAPTER THREE

Freeburn stared at him. For a moment, Tom thought the man was simply going to continue up the stairs, regardless of what he'd just said. But no. The lawyer nodded, and slowly descended.

Where the hell was Huz?

CHAPTER FOUR

Nina had been hoping for a nice, simple evening at the pub. It wasn't even karaoke night. Yes, she'd probably have got up and sung anyway, but it wouldn't have been anything she'd have had to worry about the next day. She'd have spent most of the evening bitching with Tom about the awful date she'd had the previous night, with Romit Chandra, a man who seemed unable to talk about anything except himself or his own obsessions.

If she'd shared his obsessions, that might have been tolerable. But she just wasn't as into grading different categories of meat as Romit was.

Now she was standing with a uniformed officer she didn't know in the street outside the offices of William Freeburn McNeil Todd, each of them at one end of a dead body, and trying to ward off hordes of drunks in bad fancy dress.

It was still probably better than the date itself.

"Get away," she shouted, as one woman stepped a bit too close for her liking.

CHAPTER FOUR

"Just 'avin' a look," the woman shouted back. "'Ad a bit too much, 'as 'e?"

Nina exchanged glances with the Uniform and stepped towards the woman.

"Please move away, Madam. This is a crime scene, and it's vital that we preserve it."

The spot had already been walked over by half a dozen people, and if there was a crime scene, it was probably inside. But Nina couldn't move the body. She couldn't just let people gawk at it. The woman she'd spoken to grumbled, but moved away. Nina turned back to the Uniform to say something, and stopped.

There were three of them. Big blokes, all wearing those stupid masks and even stupider costumes. She'd not seen them approach. They must have come out of one of the side streets.

"Out the way, love," one of them said. "Let dog see rabbit, eh?"

The Uniform took a step back. She was almost on top of the body.

"Stop!" Nina shouted.

Where the hell was the backup? They needed more people here. They needed Roddy Chen, who'd recovered from the attack that had put him in a coma, but still wasn't ready for work. They needed...

"Back away," shouted a figure as it emerged from the office, approached, and stood, arms crossed, between the drunks and the body.

"Why?" asked one of the drunks.

"This is a crime scene," shouted the figure. Tom, wearing a costume nearly as ridiculous as the rest of them.

The drunks laughed. When it came to authority, the

costume wasn't helping. Tom turned to look at her, suddenly desperate. The lead drunk had just taken another step forward when there was a roar from the open doorway beside them.

"Have you no sense of propriety?" the man shouted.

The drunks stopped. Nina turned to see the newcomer, and her mouth fell open.

"Well?" shouted the man. "What kind of men are you that you'd ignore the legitimate instructions of the authorities and behave like scoundrels?"

As if acting in unison, the men took a step back, still staring at the man in the doorway.

"Get the hell out of here!" he shouted, and they turned and walked away, silent. Nina shook her head in amazement as Alistair Freeburn walked over from the doorway and stood by the body, still in his costume, shaking his head.

Tom spoke first. "Legitimate instructions of the authorities? Really?"

Freeburn lifted his head and spoke as if he were addressing a public meeting. "John Paul Jones might have been a rebel. But he had no truck with mutineers."

He gave a nod, and walked back inside just as another man approached from the marina end of the street. Nina could see the uniform tense as he drew closer.

"It's OK," she said.

"I'm sorry," Huz replied, reaching them. "I was on a night out."

"You and me both," Nina told him. "Was looking forward to a few pints at the Anchor Vaults."

"I was at the King George's," added Huz, glumly. Nina stopped and looked at him more closely.

CHAPTER FOUR

"Blimey," she said, her eyes roaming up and down his suit. "Is that..."

"Armani." Huz nodded.

"I really am sorry," she told him. If he'd got dressed up in an Armani suit for dinner at one of Cumbria's finest restaurants, he'd been planning something a lot bigger than a few pints at the Anchor Vaults. Nina didn't know Huz well, didn't know if there was someone else in his life, but it had the air of one of those evenings when someone proposes.

She hoped the dead man hadn't ruined all that.

Huz was already bent over the body, taking in the more obvious details. She watched as he scanned the ground nearby, nodding to himself.

"Fell from up there?" he asked, pointing to the second-floor window.

"We think so," Nina told him, as yet more people approached.

Uniforms. Finally. Three of them, apologising for the delay.

"It's carnage out there."

And then a fourth, a sergeant, with two more people walking slowly behind her.

"Are you with Cumbria CID?" the sergeant asked.

"Yes."

"These two, they saw the mugging, over there." The sergeant turned and pointed back the way she'd come, a little way up Strand Street, by the look of things. "Well, not the mugging. Just the aftermath. Can you talk to them? Only, it's a bit..."

She gestured out towards the town. Carnage, one of the others had said.

Maybe, but there was a dead body to deal with first. And Huz was looking up at the building.

He needed to get inside. She needed to get in there with him.

"Not now," Nina replied. "I'm sorry. Do you mind waiting?" She addressed the two, a man and a woman, in their fifties or sixties, she reckoned. Both nodded.

"Time to suit up," she told Huz, as he followed her inside.

CHAPTER FIVE

Zoe glanced at her watch, then remembered she couldn't see it under the forensic suit. It had been eleven when she'd last looked. This was going to be a long night.

She'd been hoping to speak to Nicholas this evening. See if she could find out any more about his mysterious partner she'd heard so little about. She'd assumed Fox was a man, but she couldn't be sure. Nicholas referred to them as his 'person', whatever that meant.

She was standing outside the second-floor library with Huz and Nina, staring at a locked door.

Huz bent down and put his eye to the keyhole.

"You can see the key. It's in the lock on the other side."

"Wait here," Zoe said.

She went down one floor, where she removed the forensic suit. Then down another, to the reception area, and the large, wood-panelled room beside it. She knocked and entered without waiting for a response.

"DI Finch," said Freeburn. He'd changed into everyday clothing, finally. "What can I do for you?"

"Your library's locked," she told him. "From the inside."

"Hmmm." Freeburn frowned, then pulled open his desk drawer and rummaged inside. "I'd imagine you'll be needing this, then."

Having a spare key was one thing. Using it to dislodge the key that was already in the lock was another. Thankfully, it seemed Huz knew what he was doing. Either they taught this sort of thing in CSI training, or Huz would make an excellent housebreaker. A minute after he'd bent down and started waggling at the lock, there was a clunk from the other side of the door. He straightened up, smiling.

Inside, it was exactly as Zoe had expected. A library. Bookcases and shelves, packed with legal tomes: statutes, caselaw, practice guides.

Hadn't all this gone online yet? Freeburn would have wanted to preserve the printed works, too. A matter of tradition.

The walls were painted pale blue, like the outside of the building. It was a calming room. Two chairs sat in a corner by a small round table. The window was still open, and Zoe approached behind Huz, and peered out.

There was the body. Tom, and several uniforms, and a handful of civilians, too. What were they doing there?

She could see the ladder, but that only went as far as the first-floor window, more than ten feet below. Could someone have jumped from here?

"No way anyone reached the ladder from here," Huz mused, echoing her thoughts.

"So it must have been a suicide," Freeburn announced from outside the room. "Or an accident, I suppose."

Zoe hadn't realised he'd followed her up here.

"And will you look at the state of this?" Freeburn added.

CHAPTER FIVE

Before anyone had a chance to object, he was inside the room, at one of the shelves, reaching towards it, straightening a book, another book, a third...

"Out!" shouted Huz.

Freeburn stopped and stared at him. "What?"

"You're contaminating a crime scene! You're not— Look at what you're wearing!"

Freeburn followed Huz's gesture down to his feet, and looked up again. "Contaminating?" he echoed. "These are Crockett's."

He turned to Zoe and shook his head, bewildered. She pointed at her forensic suit, then at his clothes. He nodded.

"Ah," he said, and took four enormous strides, leaving him standing on the other side of the open door. "I am sorry. But really, there's no one here, and the door was locked. It's hardly a crime scene, is it?"

Was he right? Zoe turned to Nina, then Huz. They looked as unsure as she was.

"This door, is it usually locked like this?" she asked.

"No." Freeburn frowned. "We do tend to keep the key in the door. But we don't tend to lock it. These volumes." He gestured towards the shelves. "They mean a lot to some of us, but they're not exactly valuable."

"So someone could have got in and locked the door behind them."

Freeburn nodded. "Oh, absolutely. It would be easy enough for someone to get in here and kill themselves if they wanted to," he said. "Although I can't for the life of me imagine why they'd choose to do it tonight, and from my library, whoever they are."

Then he turned and walked away, his heavy tread still audible all the way down to the floor below.

CHAPTER SIX

THE SO-CALLED WITNESSES COULD WAIT. Whatever it was they'd witnessed, it wasn't a murder.

This probably wasn't a murder either, thought Tom, as he headed back inside, leaving PC Martinez and the rest of the Uniforms to keep watch over the body. But it might be. And there was someone in here who could help them figure out if it was.

Sue was still in the same room. Still in the same chair, even. He watched her from the doorway, rotating the almost-empty glass of whisky in her hands, the light reflecting from the drink to her eyes. She was...

She looked up, saw him, and smiled.

"Don't suppose I can go home any time soon, can I?"

"Hopefully." He took a seat opposite her. "I want to run through a few more things with you, if you don't mind."

She nodded, took a final sip from the glass, and placed it on the desk beside her.

"Why didn't you come with me when I left?" he asked. "I

CHAPTER SIX

mean, it was all over. The raiders had taken us by surprise. Job done."

She laughed. It was the strangest and most welcome sound he'd heard all evening. "I wish I had," she told him. "But I couldn't. Whoever tied me up, they did a thorough job of it. I couldn't move. One of your colleagues loosened the rope enough for me to get out, otherwise, I'd still be tied up."

That was odd. Odd and unnecessary. "Who tied you up?" he asked.

She frowned. "I'm not sure. I think... It could have been any of them, to be honest. Not Captain Jones. He was too busy telling everyone to be quiet and not break anything. But any of the rest."

Tom tried to think back, to remember who had been where, but he couldn't do it either. It had all been over so quickly. Like a blur. In the darkness. And he'd been focusing on getting out, getting to the pub, having a drink.

"And I don't know any of these people, anyway," she pointed out. "Not even you, until now." She smiled.

He smiled back.

"Why would someone do that?" he asked, to himself as much as to Sue. "To stop you interfering? But if they did that, why didn't they bother with me?"

Sue opened her mouth to say something, just as Tom heard footsteps on the stairs. Another man entered. Another one in costume, but no mask.

"It's true, then?" he asked. "They wouldn't let me look outside, but I heard someone had died."

"I'm afraid so, William."

William Enderby ran the group alongside Freeburn. He'd been leading the other half of the raiding group. The ones who'd ended up in the pub and tearing up the town.

But William Enderby was the one tasked with the group admin, which meant he actually knew who everyone was.

"Do you mind coming to the window?" Tom asked. "I'm sorry, but I'd like you to take a look at the body, if you can. If you can get a good enough view from up here, you might be able to tell me who it is."

Enderby nodded and approached the window. He stopped a foot away, and turned to Tom, anxiety etched across his face.

Tom nodded, and Enderby closed the distance to the window. He spent a moment looking down, then straightened and stepped away.

"Jason Knight," he said. "I don't know him well, but it's him. He's— Oh, no."

"What?"

"His wife. She'll be devastated."

"Do you have a number for her?"

"She was in one of the groups. They both were. She was here tonight. Oh, no," Enderby repeated as Freeburn stomped into the room. "Alistair, they were both in your group."

"Both?" Freeburn slumped into a chair, shaking his head.

"The dead man. Jason Knight. And his wife, Beth. They were in your group."

"Were they? I wish she'd looked after him a little better, then. Bugger's only gone and thrown himself out of the library window."

Freeburn looked up, registering that everyone was staring at him.

"And it's a tragedy, of course. But it's not a crime scene. There was no one else there. Suicide, or bad luck."

"No," said Sue. Tom turned to her, surprised.

CHAPTER SIX

"What?"

"I heard more than one voice. More than one set of footsteps. Upstairs."

Freeburn was shaking his head, muttering. Tom thought he caught the word 'Impossible'.

Sue ignored him and went on.

"Yes. More than one set, before the fall. And more sounds from up there afterwards. Inside and outside."

"Outside?" asked Tom. "Are you sure?"

She frowned, then nodded. "I think so. But definitely inside. I'm sure of it."

Freeburn was still muttering his disagreement, but Sue just stared at him, her mouth set.

She clearly wasn't about to change her mind.

CHAPTER SEVEN

It was warm in the forensic suit. Zoe was grateful for the open window. Through it, she could hear the sounds of the Uniforms, exchanging their own takes on the evening's events, and the civilians talking quietly to each other.

Who were they, anyway? Why hadn't they been moved on?

Another voice reached her. She approached the window to look down.

Chris Robertson was standing over the body, then kneeling, his head lowered almost as if he were praying. She saw him look up at the building, his gaze skirting past her and to the edges of the walls.

No point in that. Whatever had happened, the dead man had fallen from here.

Zoe turned, spoke briefly to Nina, and made her way downstairs.

"About time," she said, emerging onto the street. The two civilians looked up at her briefly, then returned to their

CHAPTER SEVEN

conversation. The pathologist didn't speak or register her comment.

"Chris," she said, stepping closer. He lifted his head and looked at her.

His face was pale, his eyes bloodshot and rimmed with shadows.

"What happened to you?" she asked.

"I went on holiday," the pathologist told her.

"Christ. Remind me never to get a travel recommendation from you."

"It's not the holiday. It's the getting back. Eighteen fucking hours, Zoe. Eighteen fucking hours."

"Where'd you go?"

"Portugal." She stared at him. "Budget airline. Don't ask."

She bent down beside him and watched as he gently moved the dead man's head to examine the wound.

He stared at the surface of the road for a minute, then back at the wound.

"No prizes for guessing what caused the head trauma," he said after a minute. "I suppose you'll want a view on distance fallen, that sort of thing?"

Zoe nodded. "We think it was that window. Second floor." She pointed.

"I can give you a time of death when I've—"

"No need. We've got a decent idea. Thanks, Chris, and sorry to drag you here."

He shrugged. "After the journey I've had, this is... Well, let's just say it's better than the in-flight entertainment was."

What had happened to him on that flight?

Her phone buzzed. She pulled it out of her jacket pocket and checked the display before answering.

"Aaron," she said.

"Boss. I hear there's been trouble in town. Do you need help?"

Aaron sounded much like Chris Robertson looked.

"We've got it covered, Aaron," she said. "And you need to sleep."

"If you need help—"

"No."

DS Keyes had been suffering from flu for nearly a week now. If he was sick enough to be off work, she didn't want him turning up and infecting everyone else. "Yes, there's a lot of drunk people about. And yes, there's been a suspicious death. But odds are, it's going to turn out to be either an accident or a suicide. Just put the phone down and get some sleep."

"I've been looking for Olivia, boss."

She sighed. Of course he had. Olivia Bagsby was an artist. A woman she and Aaron had briefly met during her first week on the job who'd disappeared soon after.

Olivia had photographs in her possession. Images that, Zoe suspected, implicated Myron Carter, a local businessman, in something serious enough for him to threaten the artist.

Olivia had been in hiding for nearly a year. They'd almost found her, once. Well, Aaron had. But she'd realised, and called Zoe and told her to lay off, and since then, nothing. And it was just like Aaron to use the time he was supposed to spend recuperating, hunting down leads instead.

"Leave it, Aaron. The best thing you can do for the team is get some sleep, get better, and then get back to work. Wherever Olivia is, she's not going anywhere."

There was a silence. Her thoughts turned inevitably to David Randle, her old boss, a criminal who'd entered witness protection, and had almost immediately broken the terms of his deal by contacting her and offering to help with her investigation into Myron Carter.

She hadn't told Aaron about David Randle. Hadn't known how he'd react to her contact with a corrupt former police officer. Aaron had never been anything but honest with her, once his initial reserve had broken. But this, she'd kept from him.

Mind you, that was nothing. She hadn't even told Carl, not really. As far as Carl knew, she'd had two messages from Randle, and nothing since. Carl was her partner, a DI whose job it was to investigate corrupt cops, and she hadn't even told him.

Forget Randle. Forget Olivia. Forget all of it.

There was a dead man here. Deal with that first. Deal with what was in front of her.

CHAPTER EIGHT

Nina glanced at her watch. Nearly midnight. She approached the window and looked down.

They were still there. The so-called witnesses to the so-called mugging. Someone had to talk to them.

Fine, then. She'd do it.

Huz didn't need her hovering about while he examined a crime scene. The boss was with Dr Robertson, looking at the body. And Tom was busy with Sue whatshername, the one who'd been stuck in her chair the whole time.

The way Tom had looked at Sue, Nina suspected he didn't mind being busy questioning her at all.

About time. He'd been hung up on Harriett Barnes for far too long. And it didn't look like Nina would be getting to the pub before closing.

It turned out the witnesses hadn't really seen anything after all.

"We were just on our way back from dinner," the man explained. From the way he spoke, and held onto his wife,

CHAPTER EIGHT

Nina had the feeling that dinner had been more liquid than anything else.

"We heard her shouting, poor dear," added the woman. "Of course, we couldn't see anything at that point. We weren't close enough. But then, well, as we got closer, that was when we saw them, wasn't it, Reginald?"

"It was, my love," said Reginald, then hiccoughed loudly. Nina took a step back. "I'm sorry about that. There were two of them."

"Yes, two. They were running... Oh, what's that direction?" The woman closed her eyes and slowly turned three hundred and sixty degrees, as if trying to recreate the scene in her head. As she completed her revolution, she stumbled. Nina reached out and grabbed her arm to steady her.

"Thank you, young lady," said the woman, smiling. It was almost as if they hadn't even noticed the dead body by their feet.

Perhaps they hadn't.

"North," the woman continued. "They were running, and they were wearing masks. I'm afraid it was too dark to tell you anything more than that."

"Were they wearing costumes?" Nina asked. The couple turned to face each other, both frowning.

"No," said the man, eventually. "I don't think so."

His wife nodded in agreement.

The pair of them were as much use as a cat on a Jet Ski.

"Where exactly did you see this?" she asked.

"Strand Street," said the woman immediately. "Just by the car park. At the far end, nearest the road. I..." She smiled sheepishly. "I dropped my glasses, and we were looking around for them when we heard it."

The woman was wearing her glasses now, so at least she'd found them. Although they seemed to be balanced at a slight angle across the bridge of her nose. Nina looked over, in the direction the woman had indicated.

That spot...

Without a word, she ran back into the building. She stopped for as long as it took to pull on a forensic suit, then continued up the stairs to the second floor.

"What is it?" asked Huz as she burst into the room. Nina ignored him, running straight to the window. She looked not down, but north, towards the marina.

She could see the ambulance. That was where the mugging had taken place.

And if she could see the site of the crime... The dead man, Jason Knight, might have seen it too.

She hurried outside. The boss was talking to the pathologist.

"So, yes," Dr Robertson was saying. "There's nothing here that indicates it wasn't suicide, if that's what you think happened. I might be able to tell you more after the post-mortem, but in the meantime—"

"Boss," called a voice. Nina turned to see Tom stepping from the building, marching towards them. She gritted her teeth. She had things to say, too.

"What is it, Tom?" asked DI Finch, a touch of irritation in her voice. It wasn't like Tom to interrupt her.

"I think we're making a mistake," he said.

"We are?"

"I don't think this is suicide," he said. "Sue's positive there was more than one person up there when Jason fell."

"The door was locked from the inside, Tom. And your

witness was tied up, bored, in the dark. Are you confident she's not just mistaken?"

Nina watched as Tom paused, digested DI Finch's words, and shook his head firmly. "If she was at all unsure, then maybe, boss. But she's not. She's positive."

CHAPTER NINE

Sometimes it was worse when the witnesses made sense.

After what Tom had just said, Zoe had to speak to the woman herself. Sue Bracewell. She was still in the same room, but when Zoe entered, the woman had stood up, finally, and was pacing the floor, rubbing at her wrists.

"That from the ropes?" Zoe asked, nodding at Sue's hands.

Sue started at her voice, turned, and nodded. "Yes," she said. "It's not like it hurts. It was just really tight. Still feels a bit weird."

Zoe nodded and asked her to sit down.

"We just need a statement from you," she said. "Not anything formal, like an interview. Just a statement."

"A statement," repeated Sue. "Good. Are you going to note this down?"

"I'll record it on my phone," Zoe told her, put it on the desk, and started the app.

Sue Bracewell was twenty-nine years old. She'd been in Whitehaven for four months, working for an accountant.

She'd been an enthusiastic roleplayer back in Liverpool. "It's not as ridiculous as it sounds," she said.

Zoe frowned, remembering the costumes she'd seen tonight, and Sue Bracewell laughed.

"OK," she said. "Sometimes it's exactly as ridiculous as it sounds. But it's friendly, and it's fun, and it's a nice way to meet people with similar interests."

"What sort of interests?" Zoe asked.

"In my case, history. I'm not an expert. I just like it."

"Tell me what you remember, Sue. Take me through it all from the moment you arrived."

Sue licked her lips. "I was in here with your colleague." She nodded. "Tom. Only he introduced himself as Alexander Milton. Sorry, you don't need to know about that."

"It's OK," said Zoe. "You tell it how you remember it."

A sniff. "Yes. Well, Tom had to go, and I was on my own in here. I heard noises. From outside. And from upstairs. Scraping, like people moving around up there. Then there was..." She closed her eyes. "A crunch, that's all I can describe it as. Out of the window. I couldn't get myself free from the ropes and—"

"Ropes?" asked Zoe.

"Someone tied me up."

"Who?"

"I thought it was part of the reenactment. I didn't see their face. Sorry."

Zoe nodded. "So you couldn't get yourself free..."

"So I just dragged the chair with me and went to the window. That's when I saw him. The body. And then your colleague, calling you. That's all I saw."

"You said 'him'. Could you see him well enough to know it was a man?"

"Not really... I'm not sure. Sorry."

"And the noises upstairs. Did you see anyone go up or down?"

A shake of the head. "Sorry."

Sue pulled in a breath. Zoe gave her a smile. "Thanks. We'll need to talk to you again, but this is helpful."

Sue Bracewell was clearly not the sort of individual who'd make something like this up.

Which was a shame. It would have been so much easier if she had been.

"And these ropes," Zoe asked. "They really were too tight for you to undo?"

Sue nodded. "Ask your colleague. He struggled to do it himself."

Zoe could check that. But she probably didn't need to.

Who would tie a knot that tight, in something that wasn't much more than a game? And why? Had it been done deliberately?

And now Nina was complicating things, pointing out that the dead man might have witnessed the mugging.

Could the perpetrators have realised they'd been seen? How could they have got into the building?

The main doors downstairs were unlocked, and the alarm system had been deactivated to ensure the raiders didn't set anything off. The muggers could easily have got in and made it upstairs.

They'd have to have been fast, mind. One of the few things Sue wasn't clear about were the timings. She'd been tied up, in the dark. How much time had passed between the main group of raiders leaving, and the noises she'd heard upstairs? She wasn't sure.

And as for the mugging, there was a record of the call

CHAPTER NINE

that had been made to the emergency services. But any amount of time might have passed between the incident itself and the call. The couple who'd seen the masked figures running away were the same people who'd stumbled across the victim, and thankfully, had the presence of mind to dial 999.

But stumbled was about right. It might have taken them ages.

Sue seemed trustworthy and responsible. But people made mistakes. And so far, Huz had found no signs of a struggle upstairs.

It would have been so easy to chalk this one up to bad luck, or suicide, and wash her hands of it. The team was one person down, and there was work to do back at the Hub. Was it right to pursue an investigation solely on the basis of the word of one woman, who hadn't even seen anything, and couldn't be certain what she'd heard?

Zoe walked to the window and looked down at the body in the road. The mortuary ambulance had finally arrived, and Dr Robertson was supervising its removal to the hospital.

A man had died. It didn't matter how busy they were, or how close the whole incident had been to going unnoticed.

If anything untoward had happened here tonight, she owed it to Jason Knight to find out.

CHAPTER TEN

Tom had told Reginald and his wife Jenny they could leave. He'd even offered to get a squad car to drive them home. But they were still hanging around, clinging to one another and looking on in confusion as the investigation went on around them.

The body was loaded up and ready to go, at least. The show might not be over, but it would be slowing down. Nothing dramatic to see, he reckoned.

Which was when the screaming started.

Startled, he turned in the direction it was coming from. South. It was the sound of a woman, and then she turned the corner from King Street and he saw her running right at them.

He stepped out into the road. She stopped, a few yards away, in a pool of light cast by one of the rare unbroken streetlamps.

It wasn't Tom's presence that had stopped her. She was staring at the mortuary ambulance, her hand clasped over her mouth. She shook her head slowly, then walked towards him.

CHAPTER TEN

"Is it true?" she asked. She had long blonde hair tied back in a ponytail, and a mask hanging loose from one ear over her left cheek. He scanned her clothing; not that dissimilar from what he was wearing. Had she been one of the raiders?

"I'm sorry," he said. "Can you tell me who you are?"

She swallowed. "I'm Beth Knight. I've... Someone told me... Is it true? Is it Jason?"

"I'm so sorry," he told her. "But yes. There's been an accident."

An accident. That was probably best.

"I was waiting for him. In the pub. I... God! How could this have happened? I knew he was a bit down, but this?"

"I really am—"

"Is he in there?" she asked, pointing to the ambulance.

Tom nodded. The body would have to be formally identified, eventually. The wound was to the back of the head; as dead bodies went, this one was presentable. Now was as good a time as any. Tom walked over to the ambulance and spoke quietly with Dr Robertson.

Beth Knight stood over the body of her husband for a full minute, not moving, not speaking, before she finally nodded.

"That's him," she said, and then, finally, the tears came.

The boss had come outside, while Beth was viewing the body. She stood with Tom, Nina, and William Enderby, who confirmed that he knew the couple. Not well, but they'd been involved in the society for a few years, attended perhaps a dozen events, were, as he put it, "the sort of people we need, the lifeblood of a group like ours, and now... Oh, I am sorry. Poor choice of words."

Beth hadn't heard. She was standing alone beside the

ambulance, silent, in shock. Someone would have to take care of her.

He looked around. No one else seemed to be making a move. He took a step towards the newly widowed woman, and felt a tap on his shoulder.

"I saw her," Nina said.

"Who?"

"The widow. Beth, is it? She was at the Vaults."

Tom nodded. She'd said she'd been waiting for Jason in the pub.

"I mean, it was chaos," Nina continued. "Loads of people, half of them wearing masks, and half of them drunk. But I remember that mask. She was there."

When he looked over again, the boss was speaking quietly with Beth Knight. She caught his eye, then looked over at the Uniforms. At Martinez. Then back at Beth Knight.

Martinez understood, when he spoke to her a minute later. She wasn't a Family Liaison Officer, but she'd had part of the training, and she'd been on enough calls to know what she was doing. She'd look after Beth Knight for as long as she was needed. She approached the widow and introduced herself as the boss peeled away and headed for Nina and Tom.

"He was down, apparently," the boss said. "Depressed."

"But what about—"

"I know, Tom. Sue's strange noises. Nina's muggers taking out a witness. It looks like we're going to have a busy night."

Tom glanced at his watch. Past midnight.

"I want you to gather as many Uniforms as you can and pull in everyone you can find who's still out on the streets."

CHAPTER TEN

"Pull in?" asked Nina. "You mean to the Hub?"

The boss shook her head. "No. We don't have room." It had quietened a little over the last hour or two, but there was still plenty of noise on the streets. "Names and details tonight, interviews tomorrow."

She turned and looked at the ambulance, then at the widow.

"I want the lot. Everyone who's out now, everyone who's been out tonight. And if we have to, we'll speak to every last one of them."

CHAPTER ELEVEN

SEBASTIAN PARSONS WAS PRECISELY what Tom had expected when he'd been told that a man named Sebastian Parsons was waiting to be interviewed downstairs.

"I really didn't expect to have to deal with all this brouhaha, you know?" he said, once he'd been seated in Interview Room Four and offered a hot drink.

Tom was sure he hadn't come across Sebastian Parsons at any of the four LARP events he'd attended in the area. He'd have remembered someone who used words like 'brouhaha'.

"I say, it's not so bad in here," Parsons commented, his eyes roaming the room. "On television, these places are all bare walls and metal chairs, you know."

"Oh, we've got a few of them, Mr Parsons," Tom told him. "But when people come in to help us, we like to offer them something a little more comfortable."

Parsons leaned across the table, his eyes wide. He was just a few years older than Tom, with short blonde hair and a poor attempt at a beard. "I don't suppose you'd let me see them, would you? And please, do call me Seb."

CHAPTER ELEVEN

Five minutes later, Tom was facing 'Seb' across a green metal table bolted to the floor of Interview Room Three, the two of them in plastic chairs.

"Oh my," said Parsons, noticing the restraints on the table and the floor.

"It's OK, Mr— Seb," Tom told him. "I don't think we'll be needing those."

Was it his imagination, or did Parsons look disappointed?

"I'm really very sorry," Parsons told him, "but I don't think I saw anything useful."

Parsons had been in the other group of raiders. The ones who'd done little more than go to the pub and frighten the townspeople, in the twenty-first century just as in the eighteenth. Parsons was the third raider Tom had spoken to that morning, and not one of them had seen anything useful.

But you had to try.

Dutifully, Tom took him through the evening's events. Arrival. Waiting for fellow raiders. Rousing speech from Captain Jones, followed by the splitting of the group. A march around the Marina, "with a little too much shouting and general horseplay for my liking, Detective Constable, but you have to give the youngsters their head, don't you?"

Did you?

And then the pub, of course. Parsons hadn't been in the Anchor Vaults – there had been enough raiders to fill most of Whitehaven's pubs, and they'd been scattered among four or more of them. He'd known nothing of the evening's drama until he'd been found by Nina and one of the Uniforms, at half past one in the morning, eating a kebab on Tangier Street.

"I must say, it was something of a shock to learn that someone had actually died. Not that I knew the poor fellow."

The others hadn't known Jason Knight, either, other than to exchange a polite greeting. The dead man hadn't been blessed with friends in the re-enactment group. But then, neither was Tom. You didn't have to hang out with these people outside the events themselves.

The victim of the mugging had woken up, at least. The hospital had called earlier. She didn't remember anything either, didn't even remember being mugged, much less who'd done it. But that often happened after a violent assault. With time, her memory might return.

Tom thanked Seb, and was watching the man walk reluctantly away from the Custody Suite when his phone rang again.

"Got a Sue Bracewell in the main lobby for you, Tom," he heard.

It wasn't until he reached her, and she smiled back at him, that he realised he'd been smiling since he'd heard her name.

He took her statement in Room Four, and she patiently ran through it all again, sipping at her coffee and politely pretending it wasn't horrible. Everything she said was plausible.

Except the one thing that hadn't made sense last night.

"So we can all agree you were tied up tight. Too tight to free yourself with help," he said.

"Right. And I'm convinced what whoever did that, did it to stop me interfering."

Sue was a witness, not a police officer. It wasn't her job to draw conclusions from the evidence. But that wasn't the problem.

"The problem," Tom told her, "is that I wasn't tied up. Not properly. They just chucked a couple of ropes across me and disappeared. If this person, or these people, were so worried about someone interfering, why didn't they tie me up, too? It's starting to look like this is more about you than about what happened upstairs."

Sue was shaking her head, a thin smile on her face. She'd put the coffee down a couple of minutes ago, three-quarters undrunk, and hadn't touched it since.

"Not about me," she said. "About you."

"How do you figure that?"

"You'd already announced you were leaving."

"What?"

"While they were tying me up, you were telling them you'd be heading off."

He had. Of course. He'd as good as told them he wasn't going to get in the way.

It would have been easier, always *was* easier, when the complicated-sounding theory foundered on the basics. And of course, there was still the fact that the room upstairs had been locked, with no one in it.

But Tom was inclined to agree. It was looking very much like someone hadn't wanted Sue Bracewell interfering.

CHAPTER TWELVE

Nina knew Lauren O'Donnell was bored because Lauren O'Donnell had told her this no fewer than four times already, and she'd only been talking to the woman for five minutes.

"This is all crap," Lauren said. "I've told you, I didn't see nothing, no one saw nothing, you're just dragging us all in to hear the same thing from everyone. Can I go home, please?"

Nina sighed. The woman was probably right.

So far, she'd taken statements from two defenders and one other raider, as well as a lad and his girlfriend who'd just been out for a drink, hadn't even known about the re-enactment, and had been more than a little taken aback by the all the drunks in eighteenth-century costumes roaming the streets.

They'd asked if they could give their statements together. Nina might have insisted on separating them, but she'd had a strong suspicion she'd be wasting her time, and if there was any way of halving that time-wasting, she wasn't going to argue. No one had seen anything. Lauren O'Donnell was almost certainly right.

CHAPTER TWELVE

"You were at the Anchor Vaults, is that right?" Nina asked.

"Yeah. So were you, come to think of it."

Nina nodded. She didn't remember Lauren O'Donnell, but the woman didn't stand out. Late thirties, medium height, shoulder-length brown hair, and a mouth that was a fraction too wide for her face.

"And look," Lauren continued, "I'm sorry the old guy's fallen out of a window or whatever, and I hope you figure it all out, but I can't help you."

The woman was being honest about that, at least. Charlie Torelli, the defender whose statement she'd taken first thing, had been just as useless as Lauren, but with one important drawback: he'd thought he was being helpful. He'd heard about the key in the door and the empty library and decided he could weigh in with the benefit of his experience.

"I've read a lot of these, you know," he'd said.

"I beg your pardon?"

"Locked room mysteries. You know the sort of thing. How did they get in? How did they get out? Are they still in there, hidden in the walls? Edgar Allen Poe did one like that, you know?"

Nina didn't know.

"So if I were you," Torelli had concluded, "I'd think about where one might conceal a body within the library. Perhaps, you know, sliced up thin?"

"We've got the body," Nina pointed out. "The question is whether someone else might have been there."

"Ah," said Torelli. "Still, the point stands. Someone else. Sliced up thin."

By that point, Nina had had enough. "So, what you're

suggesting is that someone murdered Jason Knight, and then sliced themselves up?"

Torelli shook his head slowly, his expression so smug Nina fought hard not to slap his face.

"What we've got here," he said, "is Knight doing the slicing, and then, overcome with remorse, committing suicide."

She'd terminated the interview at that point. However irritating Lauren O'Donnell was, she was better than Charlie Torelli.

"And I'll tell you another thing," Lauren was saying. She'd stood up to leave, without being told that the interview was over, but Nina didn't think there was much point in stopping her.

"What's that?"

"You lot want to sort out the other crimes going on. Right under your own noses. I had my mask nicked at the pub last night. You sort things like that out first, then maybe you can move on to people chucking themselves out of windows."

"Your mask?" Nina said, incredulous.

Lauren nodded. "Yeah. Nice little number, that, and someone went and swiped it."

"So, a suspicious death, a violent mugging, and a missing mask. I'll make sure we add it to the list of extremely serious offences that took place last night," Nina told her.

Lauren turned and nodded. "You do that," she said, and stalked out of the room.

CHAPTER THIRTEEN

"Ah. DI Finch. Welcome." Alistair Freeburn rose and walked around his desk to shake Zoe's hand.

"Look," she told him, once she'd sat down and refused a coffee. "I'm sorry about all this."

Freeburn shrugged. *"All this"* was the fact that she'd asked Freeburn to keep the first and second floors clear today, and he'd decided to tell his staff not to bother coming in.

PC Martinez was outside now, making sure no one walked in off the street. Zoe had seen her briefly last night; that had been the first time she'd come across Martinez since they'd both been injured in the hunt for Dean Somerville. "Fully recovered," Martinez had told her, when she'd asked. "And I hope you are too, Ma'am."

Martinez was probably wasting her time out there. People tended not to stroll into lawyers' offices without appointments. So the most significant consequence of the office being closed, as far as Zoe was concerned, was that if she accepted a coffee from Freeburn, he'd be making it himself. She'd seen the way the man handled minor practical tasks, and she had a low tolerance for bad coffee.

"It's fine," he said. "Really. I still believe we're talking about either an unfortunate accident, or an even less fortunate suicide, but I understand you have to be seen to follow this through as far as you can. For the sake of the poor widow, if nothing else."

Given the nature of his business, Freeburn was probably finely tuned to the needs of the bereaved. Still. That sort of sensitivity was surprising in a man like him.

"She's not..." Zoe began, but Freeburn was already shaking his head.

"Not a client, no. Neither of them. If you want information about Jason Knight's will, I'm afraid I can't help you."

A thudding noise came from upstairs, and Freeburn winced.

"I really am sorry," she said, again. "I'll make sure he's as careful as possible."

Huz was up there, continuing to examine the room. He refused to call it a crime scene, and Zoe could understand why. Sue Bracewell's strange noises aside, this wasn't even a difficult case.

But Sue Bracewell's strange noises couldn't be dismissed.

"While I'm here," Zoe told him, "I must thank you for your help in the Somerville investigation."

Freeburn looked suddenly alarmed. He stood again, strode across the room, and closed the door.

There was no one out there.

"Can't be too careful," he said, still standing. "I wish I'd been more use."

He'd sent her some documentation, a handful of financial reports that had helped establish that Somerville had turned

CHAPTER THIRTEEN

the hair salons he'd bought into brothels, staffed by women he'd effectively bought from the people traffickers who'd smuggled them into England. The corporate trail had run dry, from Freeburn's point of view. He didn't realise the information he'd given her had also provided a link to a business owned by Myron Carter.

She didn't have to tell him that. Not all of it. But it wouldn't hurt for him to know a little.

"Actually, those papers were surprisingly helpful, Alistair," she told him. "I've... Well, let's just say we're continuing to look into it."

A grin shot across his face, and it took him a moment to remember that he was Alistair Freeburn, family lawyer, and grins weren't appropriate. He was looking solemn again seconds later, but he was still standing, moving a little on his feet.

For a man who acted as if he were obstructive, Alistair Freeburn clearly enjoyed being helpful.

"One thing," he said, turning away from her to look at the bookshelves on his wall. "Jason Knight and his wife."

"Yes?"

"I'm sure it's nothing, but they were arguing when we arrived last night. I had to tell them to be quiet. We were supposed to be taking the guardhouse by surprise, after all."

"Arguing? Was it heated?"

He shook his head. "Not really. More of a debate than an argument, I suppose."

"Do you remember what they were arguing about?"

Freeburn turned back to her, his brow furrowed. "Weapons, I think?"

Weapons? Chris Robertson hadn't mentioned any wounds other than the obvious one, and that had been inflicted by the surface of the road. But he hadn't yet carried out the PM. If weapons had been involved…

"Sorry," continued Freeburn. "I mean the historical weapons. Reproductions, not real ones." He turned back to the shelves. "It's nonsense, really, not the sort of thing people should allow themselves to get cross about. But I suppose, as a lawyer, I shouldn't sneer." He picked up a book, looked at it for a moment, then replaced it on another shelf. "Detail, after all, is all-important."

He turned back to Zoe with a smile.

She was staring at him. What had she seen?

The books.

"Last night, Alistair. When you came into the library—"

"Ah. I'm sorry about that, DI Finch. I was perhaps a little carried away…"

She waved aside his apology. "You straightened some books."

He looked blank for a moment, then nodded.

"Why? What was wrong with them? Were they out of place?"

She stood, waiting for him to do the same.

"I'm afraid I don't remember," he said. "But I'm more than happy to go up with you and take a look."

CHAPTER FOURTEEN

Beth Knight arrived at two o'clock precisely, just as Nina had asked her to.

She was calmer than she had been the previous evening, but Nina could see the tearstains on one cheek, and her eyes were bloodshot and rimmed with dark shadows.

"I'm so sorry for your loss," Nina said.

They were sitting in Interview Room Four, which was probably the only suitable place for a conversation like this one. There was a tap on the door. Nina had asked Clive Moor, the custody sergeant, if he could think of any way to get a decent cup of coffee for the woman, and as if by magic, here he was, five minutes later, carrying something that looked drinkable and smelled a million times better than the rubbish they usually had to put up with.

"Luke's a mate," Clive whispered, passing Nina the drink before he vanished back to his domain. Luke was the super's PA, a man who was spotted rarely and spoke even less. And, apparently, a man who knew how to make coffee.

"Thank you," replied Beth. She was dressed in black

jeans and a dark top, but she sat erect, lifting her mug of coffee for the occasional sip as if she were at a vicar's tea party. "I still can't believe he'd do something like this."

She took another sip, then looked down. Nina turned away while Beth rummaged in a bag and produced some tissues. She was wearing her hair differently, Nina realised. It was loose, hanging over her left cheek, where the mask had been last night. She dabbed at her eyes, then rubbed absently at the back of her head, and nodded.

Time to begin.

"I know this is a difficult time," Nina said, carefully. "But I was wondering if there was anything else you could remember from last night. Anything that might help us work out what happened to Jason."

"What happened, DC Kapoor, is that my husband decided he'd had enough." Beth's jaw trembled, but she spoke clearly, and she was looking Nina directly in the eye.

This couldn't be easy.

"Had there been any indication that he might take his own life, Mrs Knight?"

"It's Beth. Please."

"Beth. Last night, you mentioned that he'd been down. Had he talked about doing something like this?"

Beth shook her head, then winced. "No. He was just... He'd stopped enjoying work. And we get on... No. Sorry. I have to get used to this. We got on well enough. I'm not going to pretend Jason and I were love's great dream, but we rubbed along. We liked each other. He always had to be right, of course," she added, ruefully, "but that's men, isn't it?"

Nina found herself thinking of Romit Chandra and agreeing before she could stop.

"Yes," she said. "I mean, sometimes, certainly. You say he'd stopped enjoying work..."

"He works for the council. County. Admin. He never loved it. It was just a job. I don't think... Maybe it was just everything. He'd been talking about saving a little and moving away, and I told him we'd have to save for a decade if we wanted to go anywhere nice, but he insisted he could find something. So he was putting in extra hours. Overtime. Maybe it all just got to him."

Stress and hard work could hit people in all sorts of ways. Beth rubbed at the back of her head again, then reached down for her tissues.

"I'm sorry," Nina said. And she was. There was nothing this woman could tell her that was going to help.

If Jason had killed himself, his widow would spend the rest of her life trying to understand why, no doubt blaming herself for things she might have done or not done that probably wouldn't have made the slightest difference. And if Jason hadn't killed himself, well, Beth had been sitting in the Anchor Vaults at the time. There were dozens of people who'd been closer to hand than she'd been. Nina and Tom had spoken to a bunch of them already that day, and even they hadn't been able to help.

"Why did he have to do it?" Beth asked.

Nina knew it was a rhetorical question, but she had to say something. "I wish I knew, Beth. I wish we could help you find out. I hope we can."

"Stupid bloody man," Beth said, shaking her head. "Why did he have to do it?"

CHAPTER FIFTEEN

Watching Alistair Freeburn struggle into a forensic suit was amusing for the first minute or two.

After five, Zoe decided to walk away. The urge to laugh had long since passed, and the man was doing her a favour, after all. It wouldn't be right to express her irritation. She headed upstairs, where Huz was kneeling in a corner, examining a wall.

"Anything?" she asked.

Huz straightened up and nodded.

"Maybe. If you look—"

"Ah," boomed Freeburn, finally in his suit and up the stairs. "Now. Yes. I did come in, didn't I? Sorry about that."

He was addressing Huz now, and although most of his face was hidden by the mask, he looked suitably shamed. He walked across the room, carefully now, watching where he was placing each foot.

A bit too late for that, but the gesture was better than nothing.

"These ones, I think," he said. The door was set in the

side of the room facing towards town, away from the marina, with the window to the right. The bookcase he was looking at was to his left, directly opposite the window. "Yes. These ones, here." He pointed to a handful of books. "They were poking out a little, and, well, you know me." He gave what Zoe assumed was supposed to be a self-deprecating grimace. "I can't just ignore things like that."

Zoe nodded, and turned back to Huz. "Did you say—"

"Only," continued Freeburn, standing almost on top of the bookcase now, "they're not right."

"What do you mean, not right?" Zoe asked.

"I... Can I touch them?"

He was wearing gloves. Zoe nodded, and he pulled one from its shelf.

"This. It's in the wrong place. It should be on the shelf below. And this," he added, taking another book from lower down. "It should be up there. It's almost as if..."

He frowned, looked around the room, and shook his head.

"No," he said. "That wouldn't happen here. My staff know how much pride I take in these books."

"What is it?" Zoe asked.

"It's almost as if someone's dropped these books," he replied. He pulled out yet another one, and found a space for it in the shelf below. "Yes. As if they've fallen from the shelf, and then been simply shoved back at random."

Dropped. Shoved back at random. How had Sue Bracewell described the noises she'd heard, after the fall?

Shuffling. That was what she'd said. Could that have been the sound of someone replacing the books?

"Thanks, Alistair," she told him. "We'll take it from here."

He nodded and headed back downstairs. Zoe thanked her lucky stars she didn't have to watch him extricating himself from the suit.

"What were you saying before he came in?" she asked Huz.

"This." He pointed at a bookcase.

The same one whose contents Freeburn had just been rearranging.

Zoe stepped closer.

"Can you see the woodwork, here?"

Huz indicated the corner of one of the shelves. It was made of a dark wood, or that was what it looked like from a distance, but closer up Zoe could see the corner was slightly rounded and a little paint had come away, revealing the cheaper white material underneath.

"It's scratched," she said. "And it looks like it's been banged."

"It's possible that was caused by someone or something being pushed against it," Huz told her. "Of course, I don't know how long these bookcases have been here. It's equally likely we're just looking at wear and tear."

Zoe nodded. "Thanks, Huz. I think—"

"You're going to tell me to focus on this area of the room, aren't you?"

She nodded. "Sorry. I know. Don't teach grandma to suck eggs."

Huz laughed as a shout came from outside.

"Have you seen this?"

The window was still open. Zoe walked over and looked down to see Freeburn standing on the pavement, pointing at the ground.

"What?" she called down.

CHAPTER FIFTEEN

"This." He gestured to a bit of pavement in front of him. There was... Was that rubble on the ground there?

"There's a fair bit of it," he said. "Bits of masonry. Look. There's half a tile over there." He pointed further along the pavement. It was the sort of thing CSI might have noticed last night, but Huz had come inside almost as soon as he'd seen the body, convinced that if there was anything to be seen, it would be in the room the man had fallen from rather than on the ground he'd landed on.

"Is there any damage to the building?" Zoe asked.

She waited while Freeburn spent a minute or two staring at the walls.

"I think so. Probably. This building has been here a long time, DI Finch. Things happen. But I rather think I'd have noticed all this if it had been lying here for long."

"It could just be storm damage," Zoe pointed out.

Freeburn nodded. "True, true. But the weather was mild last night. John Paul Jones was a bold man, some would even say reckless, but even he wouldn't have attacked Whitehaven in a storm."

He stood there, staring at the walls. Zoe was struck by a similarity. By the sight of someone else, looking up, in the same way. Zoe looking down from the same window, as the person she was looking at gazed at the building.

Chris Robertson. The pathologist. He'd been examining the walls much as Freeburn was.

What had he seen?

CHAPTER SIXTEEN

THERE WAS nothing more to be gained from talking to Beth. Nina offered her condolences again, and said goodbye, and as she was returning to her desk, her phone rang.

"You're looking at that mugging?" said Sergeant Clive 'Ilkley' Moor, the custody sergeant.

Nina was momentarily at a loss.

"The one last night," he said. "Strand Street. Just round the corner from your suicide."

"Oh. Yes."

Was she looking at the mugging? Muggings weren't usually the sort of thing the team investigated. The only reason to look any further into it was if it was connected to Jason Knight's death.

Suicide, Ilkley had just said. He was probably right. Which meant she wasn't looking at the mugging. Which meant...

"Only, they've brought in a couple of lads for it. Pair of local idiots. Want to have a word?"

"Is anyone else taking the lead on this?"

CHAPTER SIXTEEN

"Got your name on the file. Says here you spoke to the witnesses."

No good deed goes unpunished.

Downstairs, Ilkley explained what had happened.

"They were spending big, these two. Clothes, electrical goods. You know Baz, who runs the TV shop on Catherine Street?"

Nina knew Baz. He'd been running that shop for as long as she could remember. Locals joked that Baz had sold the world's first TV.

"He got suspicious before they'd even tried to buy anything. Couple of lads like that, mouthing off to each other about plasma screens and the like. Made a call, and when Uniform took them in, turned out they weren't using their own cards. Your mugging victim. They were using hers."

Ilkley beckoned her behind his desk, and flicked through a series of cameras until he found the one in the right cell.

"Christ," said Nina.

They were big. Huge heads, shoulders. Big, rugby-playing northern lads.

"Size of them," she said.

The sergeant nodded. "If they'd had any sense, they'd have just picked up one of those TVs and smuggled it out under their jumpers."

"No brains, though," Nina observed. "The mugging victim was a little old dear called Vera Marsworthy. Bit of a giveaway. Two big lads like that, unlikely one of them's gonna be called Vera."

Ilkley was frowning at her.

"Youth of today," he said. "You've clearly never heard of Shirley Crabtree."

He walked away, shaking his head, and she stared after him.

Shirley Crabtree? Who the hell was Shirley Crabtree?

CHAPTER SEVENTEEN

"You've been extremely helpful," said Tom. He couldn't read Sue's expression, as the two of them stood to head out. There was a hint of a smile, but what did it mean?

Did it mean anything at all?

They walked side by side to the exit. He didn't usually escort witnesses out of the building, not unless there was a good reason for it.

In front of them, another woman was walking slowly in the same direction. As they drew closer, Tom realised who it was.

"Mrs Knight," he said. "I'm so sorry for your loss."

The woman turned. Had she changed her hair?

She nodded at Tom, then at Sue.

Sue stepped forward and took the widow's hands. "I really am so sorry," she said.

From the side, Tom could see an earnestness in her face. A familiar look. Where had he seen that look before?

"It's OK," said Beth Knight. "I... there's nothing anyone can do really, is there?"

There was a helplessness in her eyes that was almost heartbreaking. Tom shifted his focus back to Sue, wondering how she'd respond.

Sue was still looking directly at the widow. She was frowning. And a moment later, Beth Knight gave a short nod, turned back towards the exit, and walked away.

"Tom," said Sue, turning to him. "Will you call me?"

"I... I suppose that depends if we need anything further from you. It's quite possible this is all—"

"I don't mean in your professional capacity. I mean socially. It would be nice to see you again."

He stared at her for a full ten seconds before he realised his mouth was hanging open.

"You OK, Tom?"

He was more than OK. Sue Bracewell was an interesting woman, an attractive woman, a woman he seemed to get on well with without even trying. That was good, wasn't it? He could call her, maybe see her again, outside the Hub. Couldn't he?

"I'm sorry," he said. "I'd like to. But..."

She stepped up to him and for the briefest moment, he thought he saw something like hurt in her eyes. Then it was gone, and she was smiling again.

"But what?"

"But it wouldn't be professional," he replied, almost on autopilot. "While we're investigating this case, it wouldn't be appropriate for me to have any contact with a witness. If the circumstances were different..."

He shrugged, hoping his meaning had come across.

"I understand," Sue said. "And I very much hope the circumstances *will* be different, before too long." She turned and walked away.

CHAPTER SEVENTEEN

He stood there watching her go, wondering where those words had come from. As she reached the car park, he realised where he'd heard them before.

Harriett Barnes. They were her words. It was the way she'd spoken to him, the way she'd ended things with him. The need to keep things professional, to make sure relationships didn't get in the way of what was right.

Harriett Barnes, too, was where he'd seen the expression he'd recognised on Sue's face. The earnestness. It had been half a year since they'd broken up, and every week, sometimes every day, he'd bump into her at the Hub or at a crime scene, and they'd speak cordially to each other, and he'd act as if it was just another casual conversation with just another colleague.

But it wasn't, was it? And if he carried on like this, it never would be. Half a year, and still he was seeing Harriett Barnes in other people, and speaking to them the way Harriett had spoken to him.

If he was going to get on with his life, he had to get over Harriett Barnes.

His phone buzzed. Nina.

They've picked up the muggers.

That was something, at least. It buzzed again, and the next message came through before he'd started replying to the first one.

Want to interview them with me?

Why not? He turned towards the car park, towards Sue, still walking through it. Where was her car? What sort of car did she drive?

He knew so little about her. He knew nothing about her, really.

Movement, to Sue's right, and there was Beth Knight

climbing into a newish-looking Mazda. As he watched, the wind picked up, scattering paper and sending cans and sticks rushing along the ground, lifting Beth's hair from where it fell over her cheek.

There was something there. She turned away and shut the door, and whatever he'd seen was no longer visible. But he'd seen something on that cheek. It was too far away to know what, but it was there.

He hadn't imagined it.

CHAPTER EIGHTEEN

IN THE FIVE minutes she spent waiting for Tom to show up and interview Jaden Jackson with her, Nina went online and found out who Shirley Crabtree was. In the interview room, she looked at Jaden and compared the face in front of her with the one she'd just seen on her phone.

There were definite similarities, which was unfortunate for Jaden Jackson, who was at least three decades younger than the wrestler had been in the photo she'd looked at.

"Nah, don't need one," said Jaden, when she asked him if he wanted a lawyer.

"Do you understand what's going on here?" Nina asked him.

He looked blankly at her, and she explained it again, and he nodded. It wasn't that he was vulnerable. He was trying to act tough.

It didn't help that he wasn't the sharpest tool in the box.

"You're sure you don't want a lawyer?" she asked, one final time.

He leaned forward and fixed her with a cold stare. "I seen you. At the Miner's. Other places, too."

"I know you, too, Jaden. Used to deliver papers to your place. How's your mum? Still on Moresby Parks?"

Jaden Jackson blinked, looked down at the table, and sat back. Knowing their mums, that was the thing. And it helped that Nina knew half the mums in Whitehaven.

"Can you tell me where you were between half past nine and eleven last night, Jaden?" said Tom.

"Yeah, whatever, mate." Jaden turned to Tom. "Can't be arsed with all this. We did it, OK?"

Tom and Nina exchanged a brief look.

"Did what, exactly?" asked Tom.

"Did the old bird. Vera, weren't it?"

"You admit to robbing Vera Marsworthy?"

Jaden shrugged.

"I'm afraid you're going to have to speak. For the recording."

"Yeah. We did it. We mugged 'er."

"And you admit to assaulting her?" added Nina.

"What?"

"Vera Marsworthy's in the West Cumberland Hospital at the moment. She only regained consciousness this morning. She was injured when you attacked her."

"Don't know nothing about that, pal. She fell when I grabbed 'er bag. Wouldn't let go. Alfie might have given 'er a bit of a shove, move things along like, but we didn't beat 'er up or nothing like that."

Vera Marsworthy's injuries had been consistent with a fall. There was no sign she'd actually been hit. Time for a change of approach.

CHAPTER EIGHTEEN

"I understand you were wearing masks during the robbery, Jaden. Is that right?"

"Yeah." Jaden grinned. "Thought we'd blend in."

"So you knew about the event last night, the re-enactment?"

Jaden laughed. "Signs and crap about it for weeks. Couldn't miss it. Bunch of bloody freaks, can't get a bird between them." Nina felt Tom stiffen beside her. "So yeah. We got masks. Pretended we were part of that lot."

"Did you steal the masks?"

Jaden looked blankly at her, then frowned. "What you on about?"

"The masks you were wearing. Did you steal them?"

Jaden shrugged. "Nah. Well, Alfie got 'em. You'll have to ask 'im. But nah."

This wasn't going anywhere useful.

"After you attacked Vera Marsworthy," Tom said, "did you go to Lowther Street and attack anyone else?"

"What?"

"Lowther Street. You know it?"

"Course I fucking know it."

"Did you go there last night?"

"I don't know, do I? Don't keep a record of every bloody street I walk on."

Nina glanced to her side. Tom's jaw was clenched tight. Time to step in.

"Does the name Jason Knight mean anything to you?" she asked.

"Don't think so."

She sighed. "After you'd attacked Vera Marsworthy, did you or did you not enter an office building on Lowther Street and push a man from a second-floor window?"

Jaden stared at her.

"Did you murder Jason Knight?" asked Tom.

"What the fuck?" replied Jaden, half-standing, then looking around and remembering where he was.

"Did you murder Jason Knight?" repeated Tom.

"Murder? We didn't murder no one. This ain't right." Now he was standing, and the Shirley Crabtree resemblance was suddenly alarming, more than amusing.

"Calm down, Jaden," Nina said.

"I ain't letting you bastards fit me up," Jaden said. He was looking around the room again, desperation in his eyes.

This man hadn't been to Lowther Street. This man hadn't killed anyone.

"It's OK, Jaden. Calm down."

"Nah. I want a brief now. You ain't getting another word from me till I've got a brief."

CHAPTER NINETEEN

BACK AT WILLIAM FREEBURN MCNEIL TODD, Zoe had almost given up on the phone call when it was finally answered.

"Who's thi— Oh. Morning, Zoe."

Chris Robertson sounded like someone had dragged him up from hell. Or at least, from deep and unpleasant dreams. Zoe refrained from pointing out that it was afternoon already.

"Sorry to disturb you, Chris. I just wanted to ask you a question."

"Yeah." There was a brief silence, followed by the muffled sound of coughing. "Go for it."

"Last night. When you got here."

"Here?"

This was going to be harder than she'd thought.

"Lowther Street," she said. "Jason Knight. Remember?"

"Oh. Sorry. I was in another world. Jason Knight. Your window jumper."

She nodded. "When I saw you, you were looking up at the building. Not just the body."

Another cough. "Sorry. Yeah. I was probably trying to work out where he'd jumped from. There were open windows on two floors, right?"

Even exhausted and ill, the pathologist was sharp when he needed to be.

"So it was just that, then?" she asked. "That was all?"

Another pause, then a quiet chuckle.

"Well, no, as it happens. You know me. You know what my hobby is."

It was a matter of weeks since Zoe had watched the man clambering over rock and shifting scree to recover a body from the top of a fell. She was unlikely to forget.

And this, after all, was why she'd called.

"Climbing," she said.

"Yes. Bouldering, really, but I always liked to keep my hand in. And I— Well, I was just examining the building. Just in case, you know, he'd been climbing when he fell, rather than leaning out of a window. I wondered if he might have climbed out of that window and tried to get around the building."

"Would that be possible?"

"It would take some skill, but the right person could do it."

And if they did, it might account for some fallen masonry.

"Would they need ropes?" Zoe asked.

Another laugh. "Ropes wouldn't hurt. But it could be done without them, certainly."

"Thanks, Chris. Get back to sleep."

"Sleep?" He sounded positively affronted. "I'm at the hospital, Zoe."

CHAPTER NINETEEN

Now that she listened closely, she could hear the usual noises in the background. The clatter of trolleys being wheeled past. The murmur of voices.

"Of course. Hope you've recovered from last night, anyway."

"Did I tell you about that? They cancelled our flight and made us sleep at the airport."

"Ouch. That's awful."

"That's not the worst of it. I was there with my girlfriend and her two little boys, trying to get some sleep, but of course there was a bunch of lads on a stag do there, too. And they thought it would be a good idea to make a party of it."

"Oh, no."

"Still not the worst of it, Zoe. The worst of it was that when we finally got on a plane yesterday afternoon, those same lads were sitting behind us and in front of us, vomiting the whole way back. Anyway, duty calls."

"It always does," Zoe replied. "See you soon."

Zoe hurried outside. Martinez was leaning casually against the building. She straightened when she saw Zoe approach.

If Zoe's hunch was right, there might be footage. She pointed out the areas she was interested in. Martinez listened, seeming to take it all in.

"So if you can visit neighbouring premises and check their CCTV..." Zoe said.

"Maybe someone'll have footage of a mystery climber on Mr Freeburn's office building," Martinez continued.

Zoe nodded. Good to have another PC who was on the ball. Uniform needed the muscle, the Roddy Chens of the world. But you always wanted people like Martinez and Harriett Barnes, too.

"DI Finch!"

She looked up to see Huz leaning out of the library window, beckoning.

Zoe sighed. It was only one forensic suit and two flights of stairs, but she'd lost count of the number of times she'd changed in and out of those suits and climbed up and down those stairs, and the case was less than a day old.

"Have you found something?" she asked, entering the library. Huz was facing the wall, his nose inches from it, just above the bookcase whose contents had been disarranged.

"Look at this."

She followed his finger. There was a smudge there.

"As with the damage to the bookcase itself," he said, "we could be looking at something completely innocent here. But if we are, then it shouldn't be too difficult to find an employee who's a match for this."

"For what?"

Huz didn't answer. Instead, he moved a pair of tweezers into the very centre of the smudge.

What was that? Was there anything there at all? It was difficult to make out. Huz was younger than her, of course, and this was his job.

She needed to get her eyes tested.

He brought the tweezers back out, closer to Zoe, and now she saw it.

A hair.

"This was... Well, it was basically stuck on the wall. You'd think a simple wipe would have picked it up. And this room – it's not dirty."

Zoe looked around. Huz was right; it had the look of a room that was regularly cleaned. She pictured Alistair Freeburn, rearranging stray volumes, surveying the room with the

CHAPTER NINETEEN

air of a proud father. She couldn't imagine him allowing the library to get into any sort of mess.

Huz was still holding the hair. She squinted and leaned closer.

A single hair. A single long, blonde hair.

CHAPTER TWENTY

Nina and Tom entered the team room. She looked around, expecting to see someone else there, but they were alone.

The sarge was still ill. Of course. And the boss was over at the crime scene.

If there was a crime scene.

"So now we're investigating muggings, are we?" Nina grumbled.

"No one else seemed to be bothering with it," Tom pointed out.

That didn't make it any less infuriating. The only reason she'd had any interest in the mugging was because of the remote possibility it was connected to Jason Knight's death.

"They didn't do it," she muttered. "It's clearly not them."

They'd spoken to Jaden's accomplice, Alfie, before heading upstairs, but Alfie wasn't willing to speak without a lawyer, and from the little he did say, that made sense. Alfie made Jaden look like a brain surgeon. An unscrupulous cop would have had him admitting to murder before he'd even realised what he was saying.

CHAPTER TWENTY

Tom was silent. Nina continued, "I mean, look at them. They've just about got the brains to grab a bag off an old lady. They don't have the awareness to look up and realise they're being watched from a building on another street."

"What about the masks, though?" Tom said.

"What about them?"

"They were wearing masks. Jaden claims they didn't steal them. So they got them in advance. They wanted to blend in, he said. And if they had the foresight to do that, maybe they've got just enough awareness to spot a witness and take them out."

Stealing masks. What had Lauren O'Donnell said?

Someone had stolen her mask. And if it wasn't Jaden and Alfie, then who was it?

"Wait here," Nina told Tom.

"Where else am I gonna go?" he pointed out, as she scrolled through the team inbox and found the number she was looking for.

"Who's this, then?" said Lauren O'Donnell, answering Nina's call.

"It's DC Kapoor. From—"

"Oh, I remember you." From the tone of the woman's voice, the memory wasn't a fond one. "You found my mask, then?"

"I'm sorry, Ms O'Donnell, but not yet. We're working on it. That's why I'm calling, actually." It wasn't a complete lie. "I was hoping you could describe the mask for me."

"What d'you mean? It's a mask. Goes over your face."

"Does it have any notable features, or design?"

"Well, if it helps, it's tartan. Now get out there and find out who stole it."

Nina thanked her before ending the call and turning to Tom.

"Beth Knight's alibi just went up in smoke," she said.

He turned to her. He looked as shocked as she felt. "What?"

"I saw her turn up at Freeburn's office, wearing a tartan mask. Remember?"

He nodded.

"And I'd seen a woman at the Anchor Vaults in the same mask. So that was her in the clear. She'd been at the pub when her husband died. Except I've just spoken to a woman who actually owned a tartan mask, and she says hers was stolen last night."

Tom frowned. Nina could almost see the pieces coming together in his mind.

"So she might have killed him," he said, "then turned up a little later and grabbed this woman's mask. Made it seem like she'd been there longer than she had."

And there was something else. Something Beth had said that should have jarred at the time, but had just slipped by.

Nina nodded. "Beth told me Jason was talking about saving up to move away. He was even working extra hours, so they could afford it. Does that sound like someone who's about to kill themselves?"

Tom shrugged. "You can't tell just from..."

He was frowning again.

"What is it?"

"Beth. When she was getting in her car, it was windy out there. Blew her hair around. I saw her cheek."

"And?"

"And there was something there. I'm... I'm not sure. It

CHAPTER TWENTY

was too far away. But it might have been a scratch." He stared at her and creased his forehead in concentration. "Wait."

He picked up his phone just as Nina grabbed hers.

The pathologist answered almost immediately, sounding as rough as he'd looked last night.

"Just been chatting to your DI," he told her. "What can I do for you?"

"When are you planning on examining Jason Knight's body?" Nina asked.

"Oh." There was a pause. "Well, given it's down as a suspicious death, it'll be done today. Late, though. I thought we'd all sort of assumed it was a suicide."

"I'm not so sure, Dr Robertson. If there's any way you can get to it earlier—"

"Sure, sure. Anything you have in mind, in particular?"

"Defensive wounds," she told him. "Specifically, anything under the nails."

CHAPTER TWENTY-ONE

"Sue Bracewell," she said.

Tom couldn't help smiling.

He'd known the woman half a day. It felt like years, but it wasn't more than half a day.

"Sue? It's DC Willis."

Behind him, Nina was talking urgently into her phone. Something about the body. Had she got hold of the pathologist?

"Tom?" said Sue. "Already? You changed your mind about calling me even faster than I expected."

Ah. He hadn't planned for this.

"No," he said. "I'm sorry. It's not that. It's... This is a professional call."

There was a short silence, and then he heard her chuckling gently.

Oh. She'd been joking. People told him he took things too seriously. Maybe they were right.

"What can I do for you, Tom?" she asked.

CHAPTER TWENTY-ONE

He reminded her of their brief meeting with Beth Knight in the corridor.

"The poor man's widow. Yes, I remember."

Good. That was good. "You took her hand and told her you were sorry, yes?"

"That's right."

"And then you frowned at her."

"Did I? That wasn't very kind of me, was it?"

"Well, to be honest, it seemed a little out of character. So I was wondering why."

"Oh, yes. That was it. I thought I recognised her eyes. That, and the way she moved, I thought perhaps she was the one who'd tied me up."

Tom realised he was clenching his fist.

"And do you think it was her?"

There was a long pause, long enough for him to wonder whether she'd gone, or hung up, before she finally answered.

"I'm not sure. I could quite easily be wrong. But yes, if I had to guess, I'd say it was probably her."

He thanked her, and ended the call without telling her he'd see her again, or call her again, or doing anything that might have been construed as unprofessional.

Probably her. Not good enough for court. But good enough for them to look a little deeper into Beth Knight.

CHAPTER TWENTY-TWO

Zoe had received a call from the super, on her way back from Freeburn's office, wondering what was going on.

"I understand this is almost certainly an unfortunate case of suicide," Fiona said. "I'm surprised you're getting your team involved, Zoe."

"I don't think so," Zoe replied. "I think there's more to it."

There was a pause. The super often claimed she trusted Zoe, but for someone of her rank, she kept a surprisingly close eye on what was happening on the ground.

"OK," Fiona said. "Just try not to waste time and resources. I'll see you soon."

Zoe walked into the team room to see Nina and Tom standing, waiting for her, both looking like they had something to say. And then her phone rang.

Chris Robertson.

"Zoe, you can tell Nina she was right," he said. He sounded nearly as excited as Nina and Tom looked. Poles apart from the way he'd sounded earlier.

"What?"

Zoe stared at Nina, and mouthed the word 'pathologist'.

"Oh, you haven't spoken to her? She asked me to look at Jason Knight's nails. And she was right. There's skin under them. Someone else's skin."

"Whose?"

"I don't know yet. I can analyse it, but it'll take time. And then, well, if there isn't a match..."

"I understand. Do you mind hanging on for a moment, Chris? I just want to speak with Nina."

She put the phone down on the nearest desk and raised an eyebrow at the DC.

"What's going on?"

"Tom spotted a scratch on her face, boss," Nina said. Zoe turned to Tom, who nodded.

"Her?"

"Oh, sorry," Nina replied. "Beth Knight. She's wearing her hair differently, so you can't see it, but the wind blew it away. And the way she spoke about her husband, it sounded like he had plans for the future. Not like he was going to kill himself."

"OK," said Zoe, turning to pick up the phone again, but Nina was still speaking.

"And her alibi. She claims she was in the Anchor Vaults. And I backed her up. Because of the mask."

Zoe frowned. "What mask?"

"She wore a tartan mask when she turned up after Jason had died. I noticed it, realised I'd seen a woman wearing the same mask at the pub, assumed it was her. But this morning I spoke to another woman who said her tartan mask had been stolen."

Zoe nodded. She remembered the mask, now. Remembered the way the woman had worn it. Hanging loose from one ear, obscuring her left cheek.

"And Sue thinks Beth was the one who tied her up," added Tom, and now Zoe did pick up her phone.

"Chris, you still there?"

"For the time being, yes. I do have a job, DI Finch."

"I'm really sorry. One more thing. If you were to take a climber, the sort of person who'd have the skill to handle the outside of that building without ropes, would that person be likely to know how to handle ropes?"

"All climbers can handle ropes," the pathologist replied.

"And tie knots? Tightly?"

"Accurately rather than tightly. So you won't fall."

And so the person you've just tied up can't free themselves before you've killed your husband.

"Thanks, Chris. This is really helpful. Please can you get those skin samples analysed?"

"You think you've got a match?"

The ropes. The scratch. The mask. The noises upstairs. None of it was proof, but it all pointed in the same direction.

"Not yet," she said. "But I think we might have one soon."

CHAPTER TWENTY-THREE

Nina watched the DI's face. She wasn't sure she'd seen the boss look quite so focused and angry at the same time. Not since they'd arrested Mick Halfpenny, in the DI's first week in Cumbria.

But if there was one thing Nina had learned, watching the boss and how she worked, how she dealt with criminals and colleagues alike, it was that DI Finch didn't like people trying to take advantage of her.

And Beth Knight had been trying to take advantage of her. Of all of them. And now Beth Knight was sitting in Interview Room Three, the nastiest room they had, with DI Finch and Nina opposite her, and her lawyer, Stan Basham beside her.

Beth Knight was under arrest.

"We understand you're a member of West Cumbria Climbers, a local club. Is that right?" Nina said. The boss had briefed her, told her to kick things off.

Beth frowned, as if she wasn't sure, then nodded.

"Oh, yes, I suppose so. I've climbed a little over the years."

Nina couldn't help smiling. "You certainly have, Mrs Knight. You've represented the county, haven't you? Placed highly in national competitions?"

The widow shrugged. Beside her, Stan Basham gave a snort of derision. Stan Basham liked to wind up interviewing officers by picking one of them to ignore and the other to challenge relentlessly. It was a clever trick, the first time, maybe the first few times. But they were all used to it by now.

"You were the one who tied up Sue Bracewell during the re-enactment last night," she said.

"If you say so," Beth replied. "I don't think I know who Sue Bracewell is."

Nina continued. "Can you tell me why you tied her up so tightly?"

"My client hasn't actually admitted to tying this Sue Bracewell up at all," Basham interrupted.

"She hasn't denied it either," the DI pointed out.

"If I did tie her up," Beth said, "it would have been instinct. As you've already established, I am – or used to be – a climber, DI Finch. Tying ropes carefully is just something climbers do."

The boss gave a nod. Nina reached into the case beside her and produced a mask, sealed inside a clear plastic evidence bag.

She held it up. "I'm showing Mrs Knight the mask recovered from her house when it was searched during her arrest this afternoon. Do you recognise this mask, Mrs Knight?"

Beth looked at Nina. "I don't know."

"You arrived at the scene of your husband's death wearing this mask, didn't you?" the DI said.

CHAPTER TWENTY-THREE

Beth shrugged. "I suppose I might have."

The boss pursed her lips. "Since we can produce any number of witnesses who'll confirm that you did, let's proceed on that basis, shall we?"

It was a rhetorical question, but Basham opened his mouth to object. The boss fixed him with a stare so venomous, even he fell silent.

"And this mask," she continued, "identified you as having been in the pub – the Anchor Vaults – for quite some time. Including the period that covers your husband's time of death. Because someone in the pub was wearing this mask, or an identical one, during that period. But it wasn't your mask, was it?"

"I don't know what you mean," Beth replied.

"I think you do," DI Finch shot back. "I think you turned up late, and took someone else's mask, someone who'd been there longer than you had, to provide yourself with an alibi."

There was a short pause, and Beth Knight pursed her lips and smiled at them both, at Nina, then at the boss.

"I must say, that all sounds terribly complicated," she said. "I think you're reading too much into what was really just an evening of chaos. I don't even remember what masks people were wearing. I'm sure hardly anyone does."

Her calmness was infuriating.

"We do," said the boss.

Nina pointed to Beth's cheek. "Where are those scratches from?"

Beth feigned a look of surprise. "I'm not sure. I suppose it might be the cat."

Nina shook her head. "We searched your house, Mrs Knight. There was no sign of a cat."

"Next door's cat."

Was the woman even capable of telling the truth?

"Were you upstairs with your husband before he fell?" asked the DI, getting suddenly to the point.

"No. I've already told you. I left to head to the pub, and I waited for him there, because he'd said he'd be a little while. That was where I was informed about his suicide."

The woman's eyes were wet. But people could make themselves cry when they had to. And now they knew the rest, Beth Knight wasn't even convincing.

"The office on Lowther Street," Nina said. "Where you tied up Sue Bracewell. Tell me, other than during this re-enactment, have you ever been inside that building?"

"No," said Beth, turning to stare at Nina.

"So you have no reason ever to have been in the room your husband fell from?"

"No."

Nina nodded. "Right." She reached into the case again, produced a sheet of paper in a plastic file, and slid it across the table.

"This is a photograph of a hair recovered from the wall of that room," she said. "And this," she added, sliding a second sheet over, "is a photograph of a smudge on the same wall."

Nina waited. At some point, Beth Knight would rub her head again, the same way she'd been rubbing it earlier, the unconscious movement of someone whose head was aching after a bump against a wall.

Beth continued to stare at her, unmoving.

"So if you've never been in that room, then this hair, when we analyse it, won't turn out to be yours, right? And this mark on the wall won't contain any of your DNA?"

Beth turned to look at Basham. The lawyer mouthed

CHAPTER TWENTY-THREE

something at her, his head angled away from Nina and the boss.

Not that it mattered. They knew what he'd told her to say.

"No comment," she said.

Nina continued. When Basham was in the room, every interview got here eventually. It didn't mean they should give up.

"And these books." Nina produced yet another photo. "They were replaced on the shelves, having fallen from them following a disturbance in the room. They won't have your prints on them?"

"No comment."

DI Finch took over.

"And these pieces of masonry." A further photo slid across the table. "They appear to have been dislodged from the walls of the same building around the same time as your husband fell. Are you confident they won't contain traces of your clothing?"

"No comment."

"And when the CCTV comes back from premises around that building, it won't show you climbing down?"

Again, "No comment."

Time to change tack again. Nina leaned forward.

"I understand you were arguing during the raid. Something about the reproduction weapons you were using. Is that right?"

Another glance at the lawyer, another silent exchange of advice. Another, "No comment."

"Did you often argue?" asked the DI.

Beth Knight looked at her for a moment, then sighed. "Yes," she said. She looked down at the table between them.

"Yes, what?" asked the boss.

"Yes." Beth looked up. "Yes, we did, and yes, I did it. That... my husband. Jason. He always had to be right, didn't he? And I always had to be wrong. Even the bloody weapons."

She stopped and looked at Nina, then at the boss. Basham coughed. Beth shook her head at him.

The dam had broken. This wasn't the time to interrupt.

"I studied this period for my degree," Beth said, eventually. "But did I know what I was talking about? Course not. Mr Always-Right had to correct me. Even there. In front of other people. When I knew I was right, and he knew it, too, and that was when I decided, finally, that I'd had enough of it."

Another pause. This one went on so long, the boss spoke.

"What happened, Beth?"

Stan Basham whispered in her ear, but she shook her head.

"I knew Jason wouldn't be able to resist arguing with me if I told him we should have gone to the second floor," she said. "I knew he'd insist on showing me the window there was too high for Jones's men to have reached. Idiot even opened the window to prove it. He was doing my job for me."

She laughed bitterly, and went on.

"I wasn't quick enough to take him completely by surprise, though. He managed to lash out at me when I started to push him out. Scratched my face and pushed me back against the bookcase. Must have banged my head against the wall."

She rubbed at it now, all pretence gone.

"But it didn't save him. The momentum from pushing against me was enough to carry him out of the window."

CHAPTER TWENTY-THREE

This was too much for Basham to resist.

"As you can see, then," he said, "the whole thing was an unfortunate accident. My client has explained what happened. Yes, there was some pushing and shoving, but she didn't mean to actually push him out of the window. She just wanted to give him a fright. Isn't that right?"

He paused, but only for effect, speaking again before Beth could answer him.

"But sadly, Mr Knight overreacted, and the consequences were that he effectively pushed himself out of the window."

Nina resisted the urge to laugh. She'd heard some bad defences in her time, but surely no one would buy this one?

"I'm sorry," said Beth, "but that's not what happened."

"It isn't?" asked the boss. Stan Basham's head dropped, his face in his hands.

Beth swallowed. "No." A shake of the head. "It was me. I pushed Jason out of the window. He just finished the job."

CHAPTER TWENTY-FOUR

"So, not a suicide, then," Fiona said, leaning back and fixing Zoe with a serious gaze.

"No."

"It seems I was right to trust you."

As an attempt to steal the credit, that was breathtaking by anyone's standards, but it wasn't like Zoe could do anything about it. And... was that the faintest hint of a smile on the super's face?

She was joking, then. You couldn't always tell with Fiona. But this time, yes. She was joking.

"Well done, Zoe. Persistence, intuition, delegation. I should probably congratulate myself on recruiting you, too, but that's nearly a year ago now, and I can't dine out on that for much longer. How's your DS?"

Again with the detail. For a detective superintendent to be aware that a detective sergeant was off work, sick – not with anything serious, either – wasn't just unusual. It was bizarre.

But that was the way Fiona operated. Sometimes, she'd

CHAPTER TWENTY-FOUR

float about, dealing with rarefied matters, budgets, the Assistant Chief Constable. And sometimes she'd wonder how Aaron was.

Zoe had just spoken to Aaron, as it happened.

"He says he'll be back in tomorrow. He sounds a lot better. I'll tell him you asked after him."

"Please do," Fiona said.

Aaron had sounded physically healthier. He'd neither coughed nor sneezed for the duration of their six-minute call, and he'd assured her he was feeling fine.

But he'd sounded down. Depressed. He'd been a serious man for the ten or so months Zoe had known him, but there had always been a spark.

Zoe hadn't seen that spark in him for weeks. Maybe it would be there when he returned to work. Maybe it wouldn't.

"There's something else," she said. She'd been mulling it over for a while now, deciding to ask, changing her mind, changing it again.

But she'd gone as far as she could.

"The papers I got from Alistair Freeburn."

Fiona nodded. "The ones about that salon, Dean whatshisname, yes?"

"That's right." It wasn't one salon, it was a whole chain of them, and Dean Somerville had been running them as brothels staffed by women who were little more than slaves, but Fiona knew all that. "Alistair provided me with some paperwork about a number of his clients that was very useful."

"Useful how?" Fiona asked.

This was why Zoe had delayed. This was the moment where she had to trust Fiona, or back away and say nothing.

And if she backed away and said nothing, she might as well give up and go home.

"Useful in linking Dean Somerville's operation with local organised crime."

She stopped. The two of them looked at one another in silence.

Local organised crime. Fiona had to know that meant one man, and one man alone.

Myron Carter.

"But," Zoe continued, "I've gone as far as I can with it. I think I can make the links, but not to the standard I'd need to make an arrest, much less bring a charge."

"Is that because the evidence isn't strong enough? Because if you're asking me for more people to find out more things, well, there's two problems there. One of them is resources. And the other, well, I think you know what the other is. He's a big guy, he wears nice suits, and he doesn't like you working cases in his territory."

DI Ralph Streeting. He ran Specialist Crime and Intel, which put him on point when it came to organised crime. Zoe thought the super had done as good a job as she could of keeping the man off her back. But Zoe knew it was worse than that.

Because Zoe was absolutely convinced Ralph Streeting was in Myron Carter's pocket.

She wasn't supposed to be investigating Carter. But if she ever handed her investigation of Carter to anyone, it wouldn't be Ralph Streeting.

"It's not about more evidence," Zoe told the super. "It's about more expert analysis of the evidence we've got."

"Meaning?"

"I'd like to bring in a forensic accountant. Ideally from

another force. I know there's a cost issue, but I'm not talking about taking on a full-time employee. We simply borrow someone from another force for a limited number of hours. It'll cost us, yes. But not much."

Fiona nodded. "You're good with numbers, Zoe. It's one of the things they said about you in the Midlands. You think you've gone as far as you can?"

"I need someone whose job it is to do this. And I need them on the quiet. No one can know."

Fiona eyed her. "I can't promise anything, but you've made a decent argument. Leave it with me."

Zoe thanked the super and left, passing her assistant, Luke, on the way out and back down to her own office.

She sank into her chair and called Carl. She'd caught a murderer and might just have convinced Fiona to hire a forensic accountant.

There were so many things she couldn't tell Carl at the moment. It was nice to find something she could.

We hope you enjoyed reading *The Raid*. The story continues in Cumbria Crime book 4, *The Barn*, in which Zoe and the team must solve a murder of a student who has been stabbed to death outside a burning barn.

Buy from book retailers or via the Rachel McLean website.

Rachel and Joel

CUMBRIA CRIME BOOK 4, THE BARN

DI Zoe Finch has been working in Cumbria for a year. She's finally got to grips with her team, the area and much of its criminal underworld.

But when a young student is found stabbed to death outside a burning barn, the investigation leads her both out of Cumbria and closer to home. Why was the victim there? Who was he with? And is the murder linked to other cases her team have worked on?

The click is ticking and the killer isn't done with Cumbria yet. There's more blood to be shed, and it might be someone Zoe knows.

Buy from book retailers or via the Rachel McLean website.

READ THE CUMBRIA CRIME SERIES

The Harbour

The Mine

The Cairn

The Barn

The Lake

The Wood

...and more to come

Buy from book retailers or via the Rachel McLean website.

ALSO BY RACHEL MCLEAN

The DI Zoe Finch Series – buy from book retailers or via the Rachel McLean website.

Deadly Wishes

Deadly Choices

Deadly Desires

Deadly Terror

Deadly Reprisal

Deadly Fallout

Deadly Christmas

Deadly Origins, the FREE Zoe Finch prequel

The Dorset Crime Series – buy from book retailers or via the Rachel McLean website.

The Corfe Castle Murders

The Clifftop Murders

The Island Murders

The Monument Murders

The Millionaire Murders

The Fossil Beach Murders

The Blue Pool Murders

The Lighthouse Murders

The Ghost Village Murders

The Poole Harbour Murders

...and more to come

The Ballard Down Murder, the FREE Dorset Crime prequel

The McBride & Tanner Series – Buy from book retailers or via the Rachel McLean website.

Blood and Money

Death and Poetry

Power and Treachery

Secrets and History

Read the London Cosy Mystery Series by Rachel McLean and Millie Ravensworth – Buy from book retailers or via the Rachel McLean website.

Death at Westminster

Death in the West End

Death at Tower Bridge

Death on the Thames

Death at St Paul's Cathedral

Death at Abbey Road

The Lyme Regis Women's Swimming Club series by Rachel McLean and Millie Ravensworth – buy from book retailers or via the Rachel McLean website.

The Lyme Regis Women's Swimming Club

A Brush with Death

...and more to come

ALSO BY JOEL HAMES

The Sam Williams Series – Buy now in ebook, paperback and audiobook

Dead North

No One Will Hear

The Cold Years

The Art of Staying Dead

Victims, a Sam Williams novella

Caged, a Sam Williams short

, Croydon, CR0 4YY